Jake Goes to Soccer Practice

A Book about Telling Time

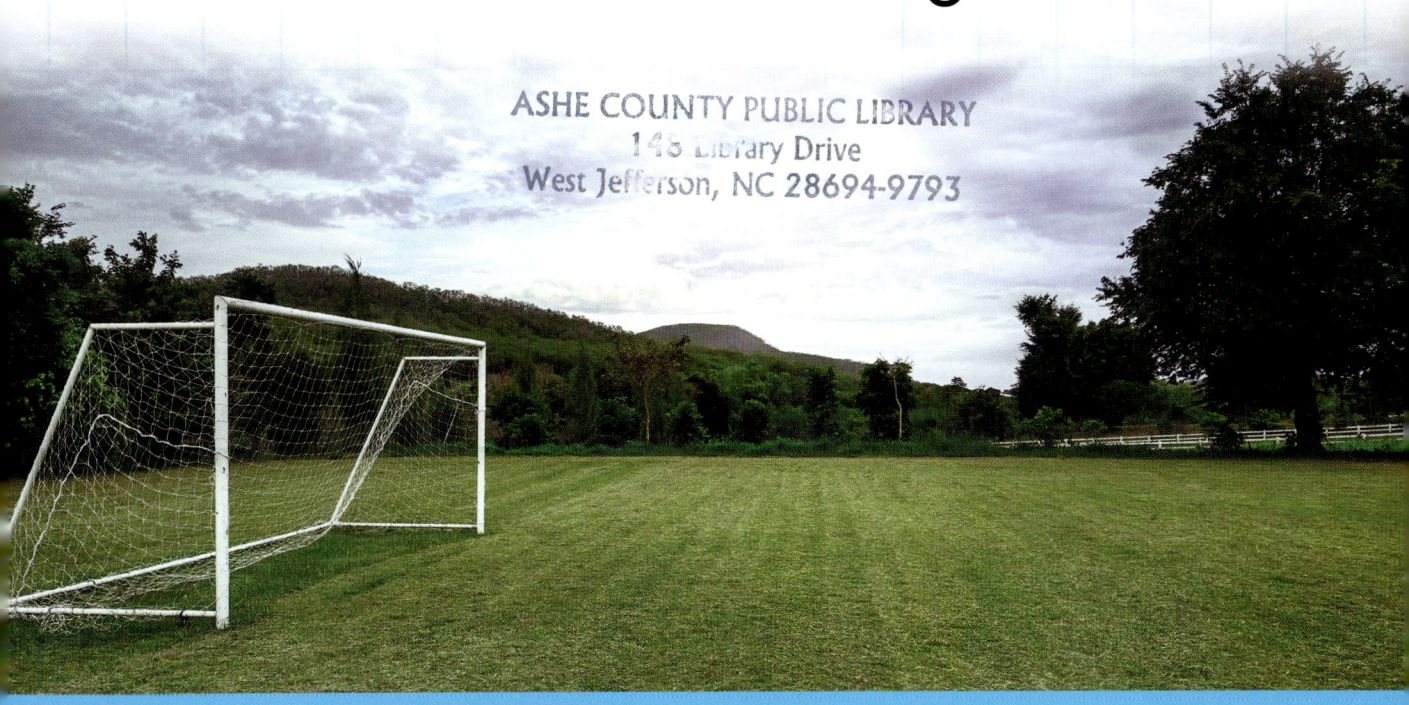

BY CHARLY HALEY

![The Child's World - childsworld.com]

Published by The Child's World®
1980 Lookout Drive • Mankato, MN 56003-1705
800-599-READ • www.childsworld.com

Photographs ©: Shutterstock Images, cover (foreground), cover (background), 1, 2, 3, 6, 7 (background), 8 (background), 17, 20, 23; iStockphoto, 4, 12, 19; T. Salamatik/Shutterstock Images, 7 (watch face), 8 (watch face); Dmitry Zimin/Shutterstock Images, 9, 11, 15

Copyright © 2019 by The Child's World®
All rights reserved. No part of this book may be reproduced or utilized in any form or by any means without written permission from the publisher.

ISBN HARDCOVER: 9781503824911
ISBN PAPERBACK: 9781622434251
LCCN 2017964158

Printed in the United States of America
PA02387

About the Author

Charly Haley is a writer and children's book editor who lives in Minnesota. Aside from reading and writing, she enjoys music, yoga, and spending time with friends and family.

Today was a big day for Jake. What did Jake do today?

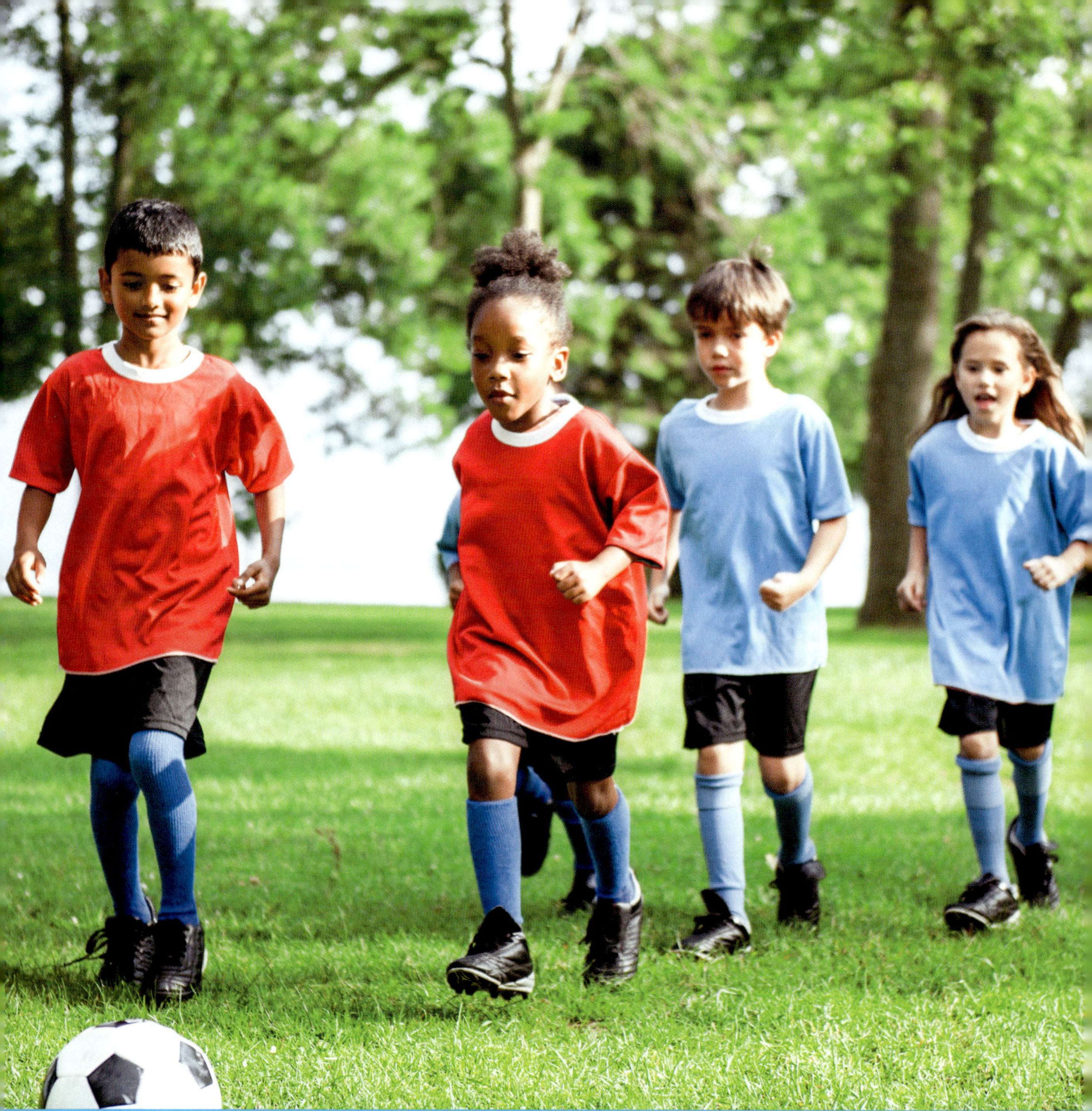

Jake went to soccer practice. His parents dropped him off. They asked when they should pick Jake up.

Jake looked at his watch. The short hand points to the **hour**. The long hand points to the **minute**.

7

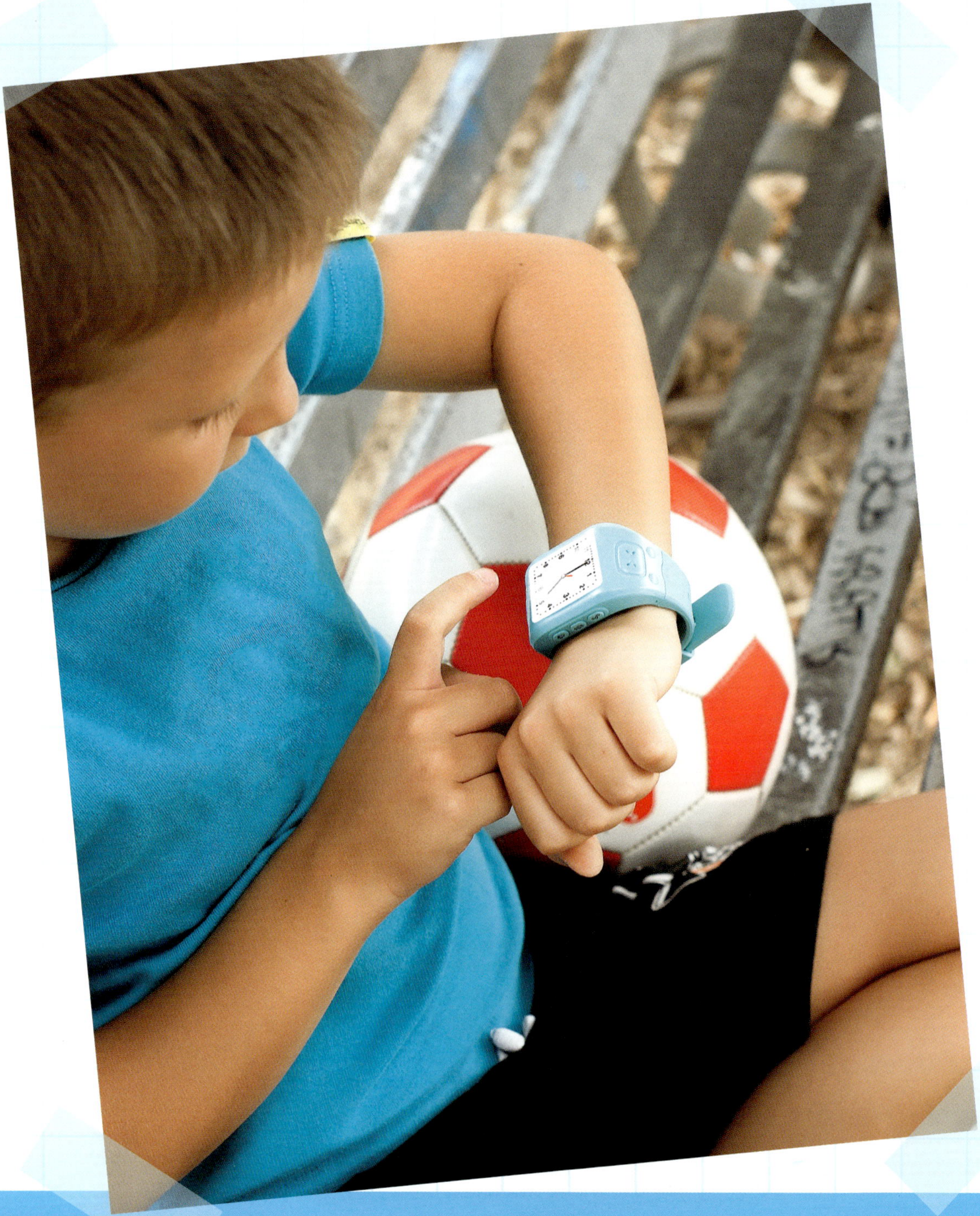

The short hand pointed to the 5. The long hand pointed to the 12. It was five **o'clock**.

There are 60 minutes in one hour. Each number on the clock stands for five minutes.

11 12 1 2 3 4 5 6 7 8 9 10

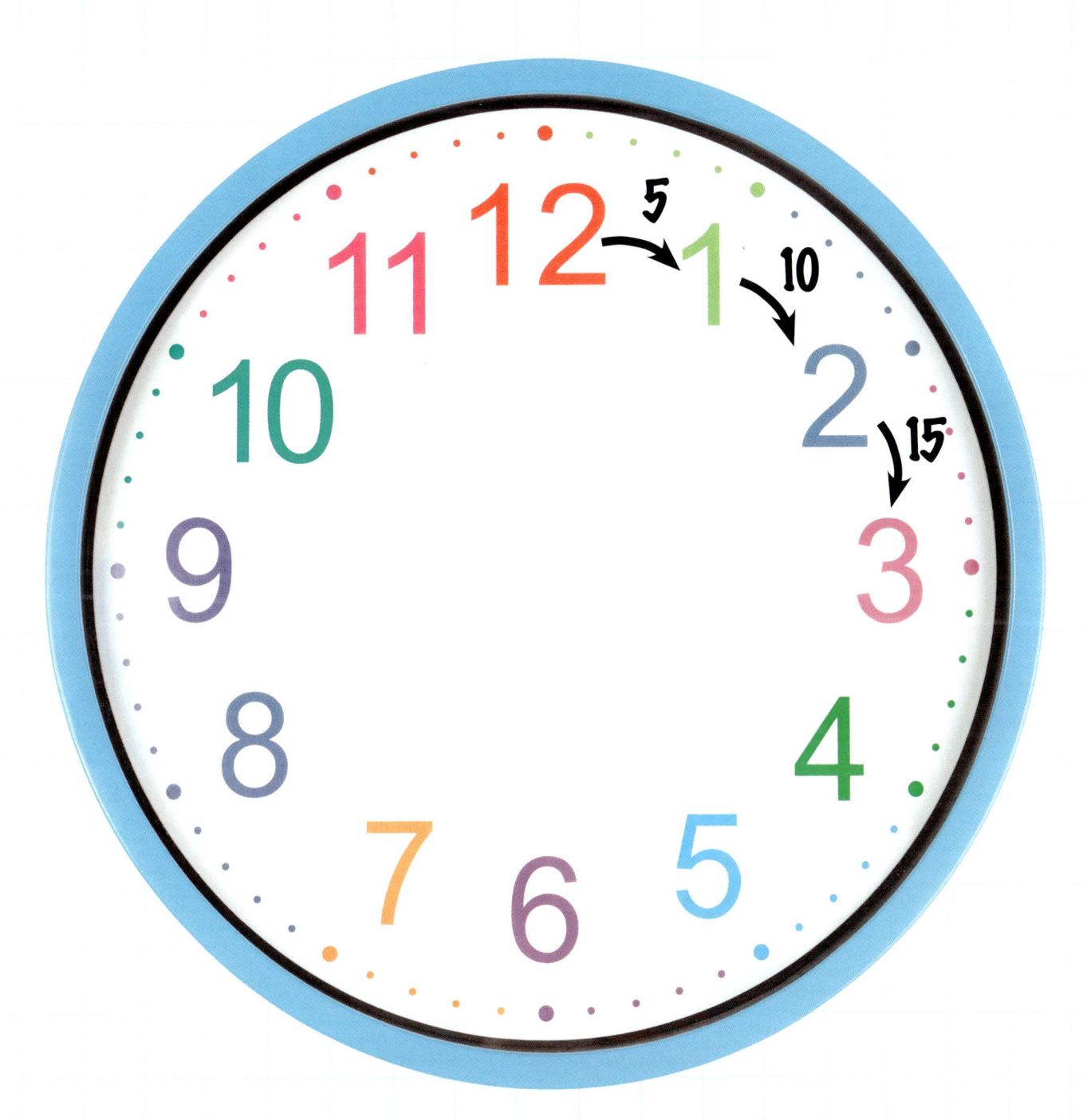

5
10
15

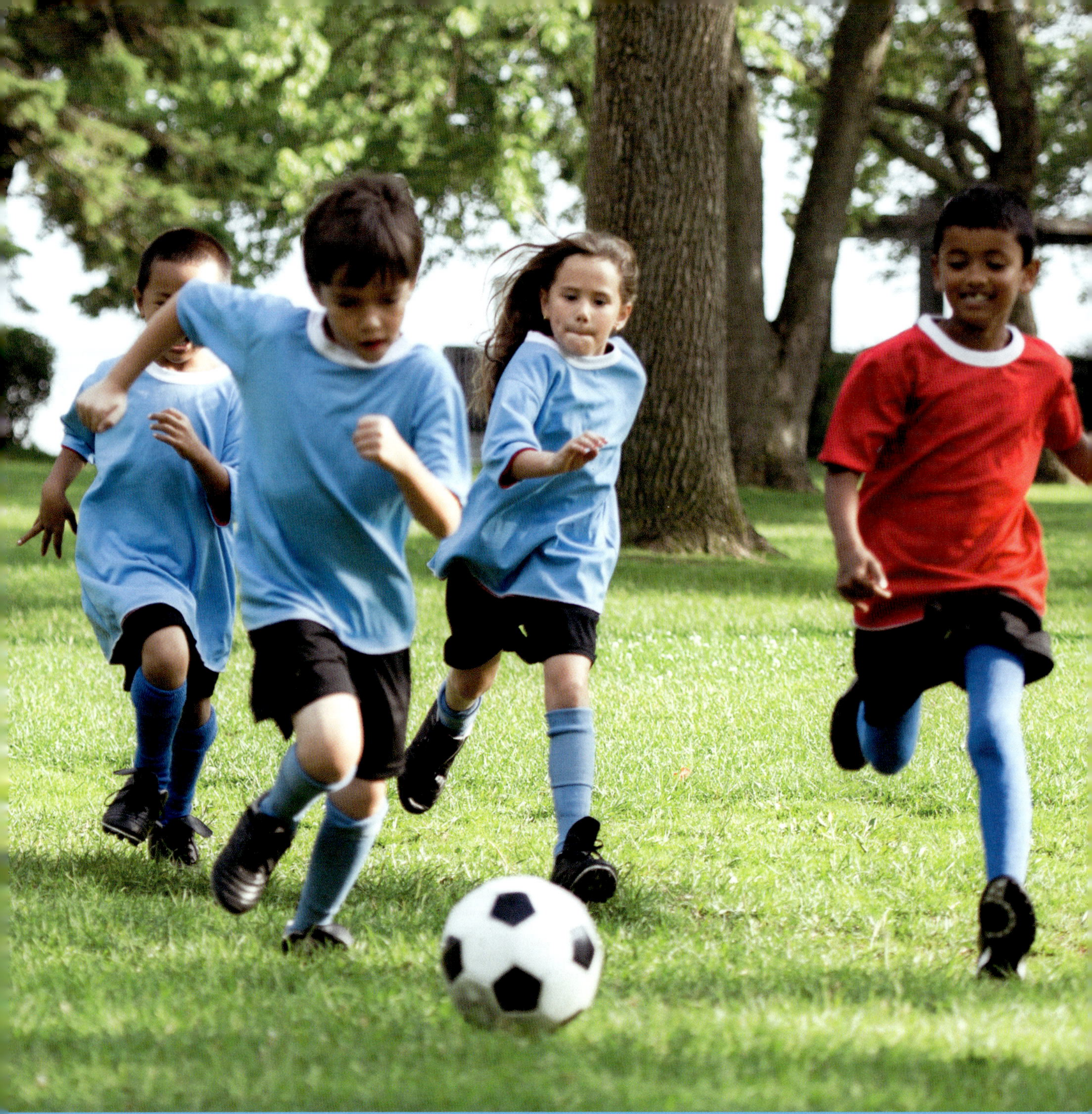

Soccer practice would end at 6:15. Jake told his parents to pick him up then.

At 6:15, soccer practice was over. The short hand pointed to the 6. The long hand pointed to the 3.

long hand

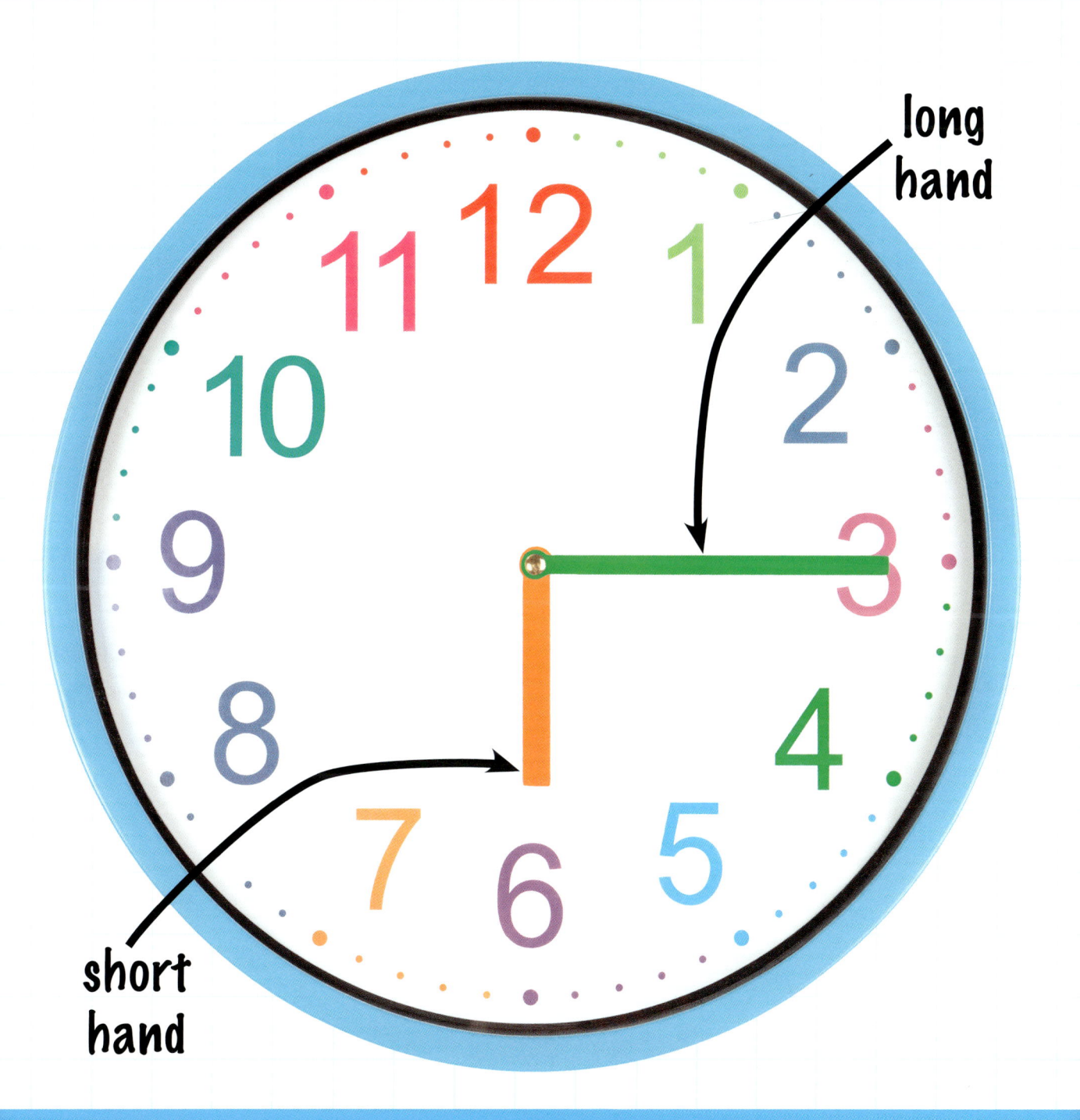

short hand

15

Jake had a great time!

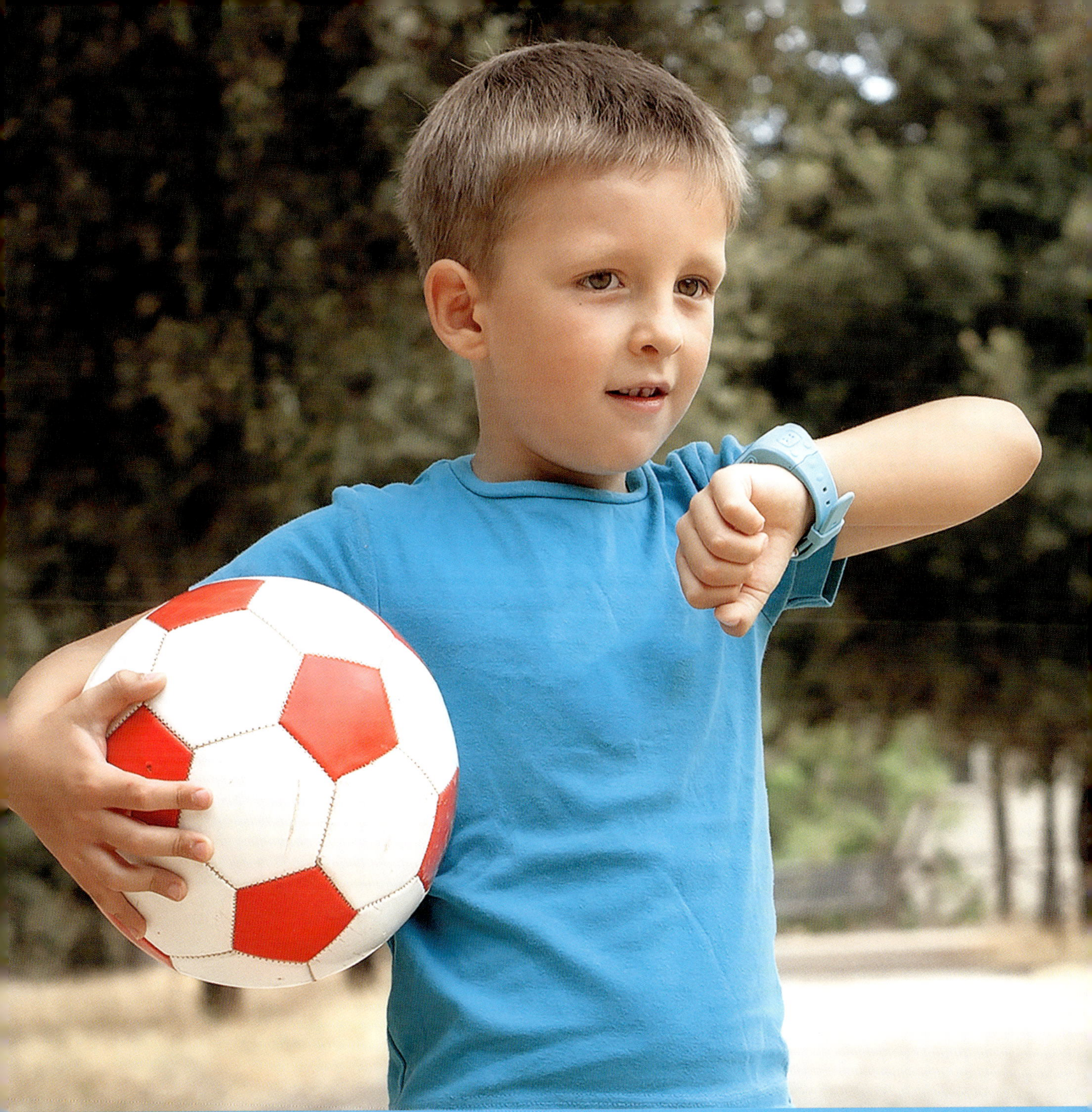

Jake's parents were right on time to pick him up.

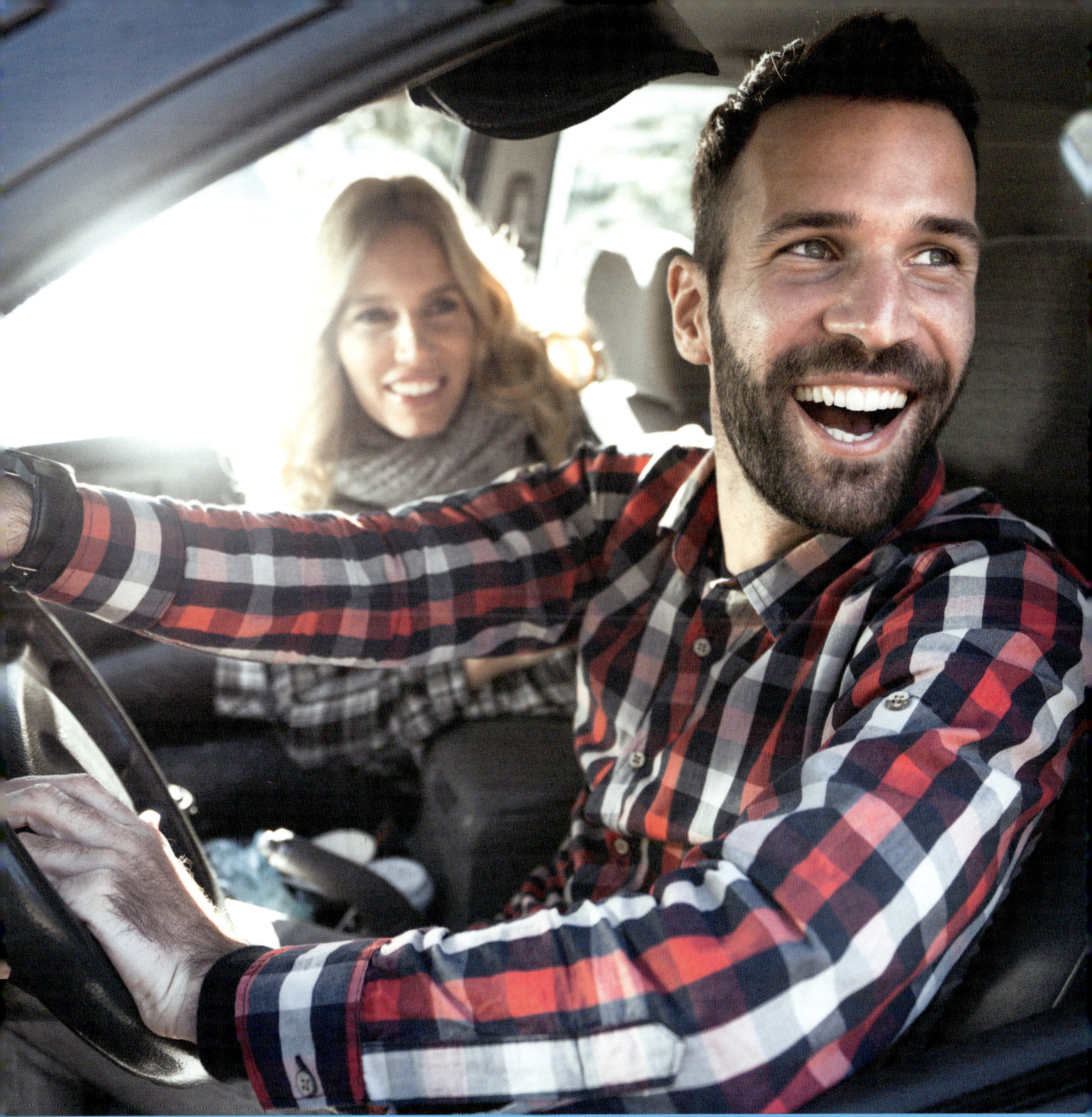

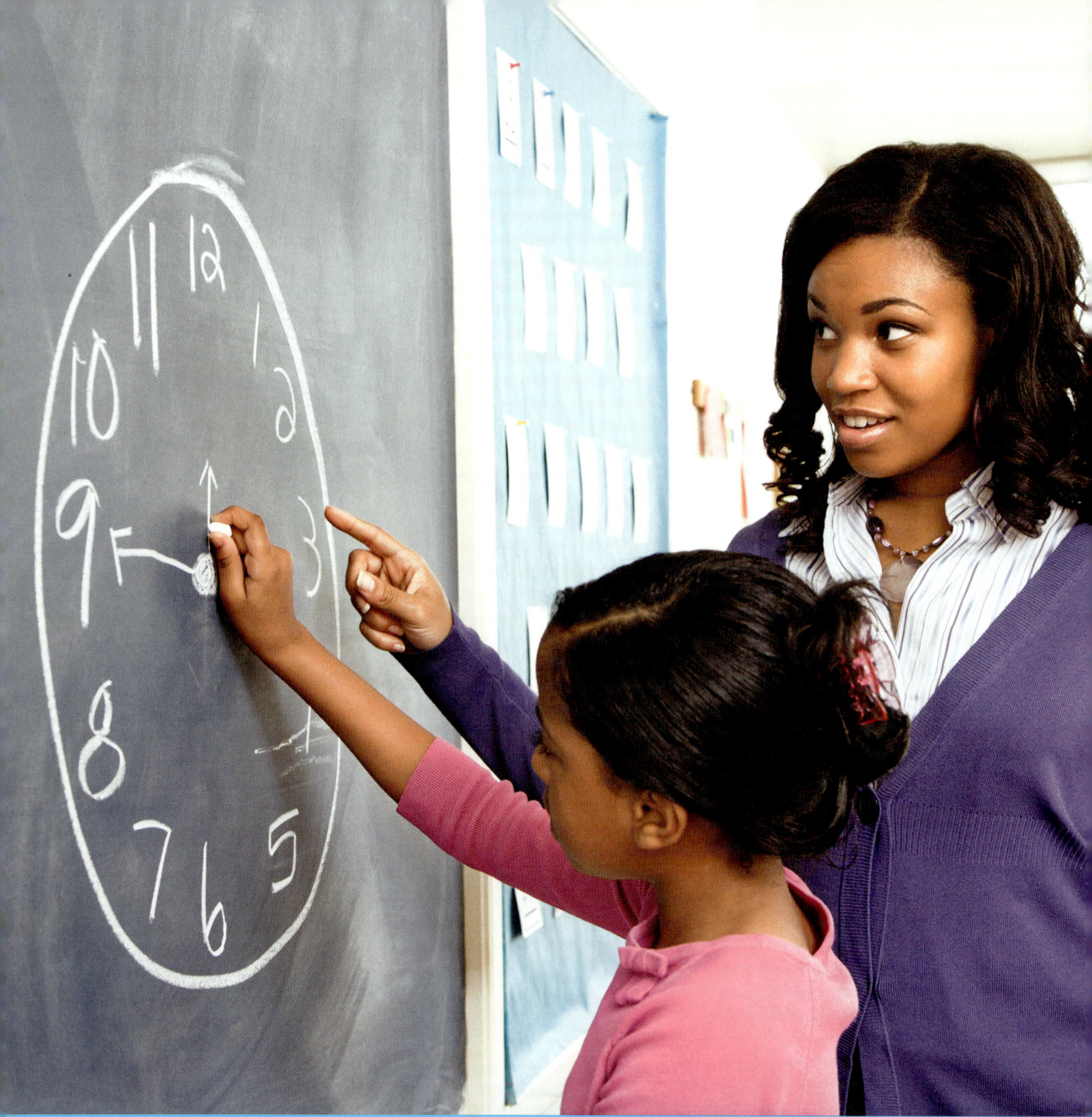

When do you

have to tell time?

Words to Know

hour (OWR) An hour is a long period of time that lasts 60 minutes. The short hand on a clock points to the hour.

minute (MIN-it) A minute is a short period of time that lasts 60 seconds. The long hand on a clock points to the minute.

o'clock (uh-KLOK) O'clock is a word used to say what hour it is in the day. Jake's soccer practice started at five o'clock.

Extended Learning Activities

1. Why is it important to be able to tell time?

2. Hours and minutes are just some of the words used to talk about time. What other words do people use to talk about time?

3. Being "on time" means being somewhere when you are supposed to be there. Why might it be important to be on time?

To Learn More

Books

Cousins, Lucy. *Maisy's First Clock*. Somerville, MA: Candlewick Press, 2011.

Davies, Kate. *Tick Tock Tell the Time*. Hauppauge, NY: Barron's Educational Series, 2017.

Shaw, Gina. *Tick-Tock! Measuring Time*. New York, NY: Penguin Young Readers, 2018.

Web Sites

Visit our Web site for links about telling time:
childsworld.com/links

Note to Parents, Teachers, and Librarians: We routinely verify our Web links to make sure they are safe and active sites. So encourage your readers to check them out!

ER
HAL

5/29/19